W9-AHM-340

Moonlight
on the
Magic Flute

Magic Tree House® Books

#1: Dinosaurs Before Dark
#2: The Knight at Dawn
#3: Mummies in the Morning
#4: Pirates Past Noon
#5: Night of the Ninjas
#6: Afternoon on the Amazon
#7: Sunset of the Sabertooth
#8: Midnight on the Moon
#9: Dolphins at Daybreak
#10: Ghost Town at Sundown
#11: Lions at Lunchtime
#12: Polar Bears Past Bedtime
#13: Vacation Under the Volcano
#14: Day of the Dragon King
#15: Viking Ships at Sunrise
#16: Hour of the Olympics
#17: Tonight on the *Titanic*
#18: Buffalo Before Breakfast
#19: Tigers at Twilight
#20: Dingoes at Dinnertime
#21: Civil War on Sunday
#22: Revolutionary War on Wednesday
#23: Twister on Tuesday
#24: Earthquake in the Early Morning
#25: Stage Fright on a Summer Night
#26: Good Morning, Gorillas
#27: Thanksgiving on Thursday
#28: High Tide in Hawaii

Merlin Missions

#29: Christmas in Camelot
#30: Haunted Castle on Hallows Eve
#31: Summer of the Sea Serpent
#32: Winter of the Ice Wizard
#33: Carnival at Candlelight
#34: Season of the Sandstorms
#35: Night of the New Magicians
#36: Blizzard of the Blue Moon
#37: Dragon of the Red Dawn
#38: Monday with a Mad Genius
#39: Dark Day in the Deep Sea
#40: Eve of the Emperor Penguin

Magic Tree House® Research Guides

Dinosaurs
Knights and Castles
Mummies and Pyramids
Pirates
Rain Forests
Space
Titanic
Twisters and Other Terrible Storms
Dolphins and Sharks
Ancient Greece and the Olympics
American Revolution
Sabertooths and the Ice Age
Pilgrims
Ancient Rome and Pompeii
Tsunamis and Other Natural Disasters
Polar Bears and the Arctic
Sea Monsters
Penguins and Antarctica
New! Leonardo da Vinci

MAGIC TREE HOUSE® #41
A MERLIN MISSION

by Mary Pope Osborne

illustrated by Sal Murdocca

SCHOLASTIC INC.
New York Toronto London Auckland
Sydney Mexico City New Delhi Hong Kong

ISBN 978-0-545-30227-2

Published by Scholastic Inc., 557 Broadway, New York, NY 10012, by arrangement with Random House Children's Books, a division of Random House, Inc.

12 11 10 9 8 7 6 5 4 3 2 1 12 13 14 15/0

Printed in the U.S.A. 40

First Scholastic printing, September 2010

To Janet, Alan, Colin, and Ross,
who have known for a long time
that music is magic

And with special thanks
to Dr. Jack Hrkach

Dear Reader,

I've always wanted Jack and Annie to go to the country of Austria, and now, finally, they do in Moonlight on the Magic Flute. *When I was a small child, my family lived in Austria for three years. Our home was in Salzburg, a beautiful old town situated on the banks of a river and surrounded by mountains. Best of all, a huge castle sits on a hilltop in Salzburg overlooking the town. I could see the castle from the windows of our house!*

Living in Austria was like living in a fairy tale. I'm certain it gave me my love of fairy tales and folklore, and it also gave me the feeling from a very early age that everyday life has a touch of magic to it. So I hope that now you, too, will have a great trip to this country that meant so much to me a long time ago.

Mary Pope Osborne

CONTENTS

"I watched the music turn to light."
—Sara Teasdale, *A Minuet of Mozart's*

Prologue

One summer day in Frog Creek, Pennsylvania, a mysterious tree house appeared in the woods. A brother and sister named Jack and Annie soon learned that the tree house was magic—it could take them to any time and any place in history. They also learned that the tree house belonged to Morgan le Fay, a magical librarian from the legendary realm of Camelot.

After Jack and Annie traveled on many adventures for Morgan, Merlin the magician began sending them on "Merlin Missions" in the tree house. With help from two young sorcerers named Teddy and Kathleen, Jack and Annie visited four *mythical* places and found valuable objects to help save Camelot.

On their next eight Merlin Missions, Jack and Annie once again traveled to *real* times and *real* places in history: Venice, Baghdad, Paris, New

York City, Tokyo, Florence, the deep ocean, and Antarctica. After proving to Merlin that they could use magic wisely, they were awarded the Wand of Dianthus, a powerful magic wand that helped them make their own magic. With the wand, Jack and Annie were able to find four secrets of happiness to help Merlin when he was in trouble.

Now Jack and Annie are waiting to hear from Merlin again. . . .

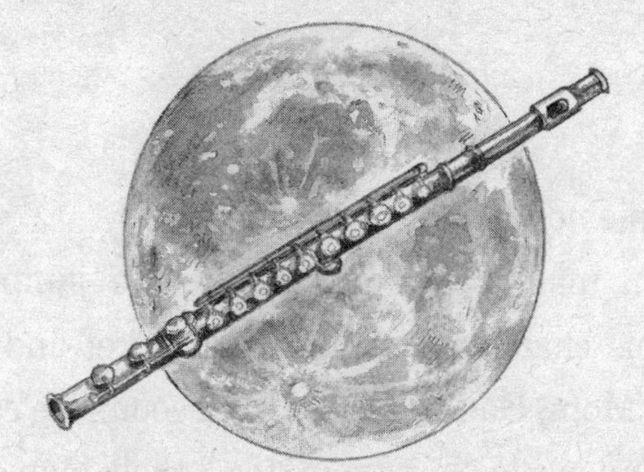

CHAPTER ONE

To the Summer Palace

Jack was sitting at the computer in the living room. He was doing research on penguins for a school project. His mom and dad were cooking in the kitchen. Jack could smell bread baking in the oven and spaghetti sauce bubbling on top of the stove.

"Jack!" Annie burst into the living room. "Come with me!" she said.

"What's going on?" said Jack.

"They're here!" said Annie.

"Teddy? Kathleen?" asked Jack.

Annie nodded, her eyes shining.

"Oh, man!" Jack whispered. He jumped up from his chair and grabbed his jacket and backpack. "Mom, Dad—we'll be back soon!" he called.

"Dinner's in thirty minutes," their mom called from the kitchen.

"No problem!" said Annie. Then she and Jack headed out the front door into the cool spring air.

"Where did you see them?" said Jack.

"At the edge of the woods!" said Annie. "I was riding my bike home from my piano lesson. When they saw me, they waved."

"You didn't stop and talk to them?" said Jack.

"No, I pointed to the house," said Annie, "to let them know I had to get you first."

"Oh! Thanks!" said Jack. "We'd better hurry!"

"I wonder where they're sending us!" said Annie as they crossed their yard and headed up the sidewalk. "I wonder what our next mission is! Hey, did you bring the Wand of Dianthus?"

"Yep, it's in my backpack!" said Jack.

Jack and Annie ran into the Frog Creek woods. They hurried through the shadowy light of late afternoon, until they came to the tallest tree. Jack looked up. The tree house *was* back. The two young enchanters from Camelot were looking out the window.

"Hi!" yelled Jack and Annie.

"Hello!" Teddy and Kathleen shouted.

Annie grabbed the rope ladder and climbed up into the tree house. Jack followed.

"We're so glad you're back!" said Annie. She hugged Teddy and Kathleen. Jack hugged them, too.

"How's Penny?" Jack asked. He'd been missing the little penguin they had given Merlin on their last adventure.

"Oh, Penny and Merlin have become the best of friends," said Kathleen. "She has brought him much joy and laughter."

"Cool," said Jack. He wasn't surprised. Penny had made him really happy, too.

"What do you want us to do now?" said Annie.

"On your last missions, you found secrets of happiness to help Merlin," said Kathleen.

Jack and Annie nodded.

"Now, on your next mission, Merlin wants you to help bring happiness to *millions* of people," said Kathleen.

"Whoa," said Jack. "That's a big job."

Teddy and Kathleen laughed.

"How do we do that?" asked Jack.

"Simple," said Teddy. "You must seek out a brilliant artist—"

"Do you mean like a painter?" asked Annie.

"It could be," said Teddy. "But it could also be any person who uses passion and imagination to create something beautiful."

"Merlin wants you to help put that artist on the right path," said Teddy, "to share his or her gifts with the world."

"Oh, cool!" said Annie. "Where do we start?"

Kathleen took a creamy white envelope from

her cloak. It was sealed with melted red wax. In fancy writing, it said: *For Jack and Annie of Frog Creek.* "'Tis a royal invitation," said Kathleen.

Jack took the envelope. He carefully broke the seal and pulled out a thick card with gold edges and gold script. He read aloud:

You are invited to a party
at the Summer Palace
October 13, 1762
five o'clock in the evening

"A party at a summer palace! In 1762!" said Annie.

"Yes," said Teddy. "The palace is in Vienna, Austria. It is one of the most splendid palaces in all the world."

"That sounds like fun," said Annie.

"Indeed, it should be," said Kathleen. "But you must watch your manners. And beware of unexpected dangers."

"What kind of dangers?" asked Jack.

"I do not know," said Kathleen. "But Merlin believes you will need magic to keep safe. Did you bring the Wand of Dianthus?"

"Yes," said Jack. He reached into his backpack and pulled out the silvery wand. It was shaped like the horn of a unicorn.

Kathleen took the wand from Jack. She closed her eyes and spun it through the air, as if she were spinning a baton. In a blur of light and movement, the wand changed into a small silver flute.

"Wow," said Annie.

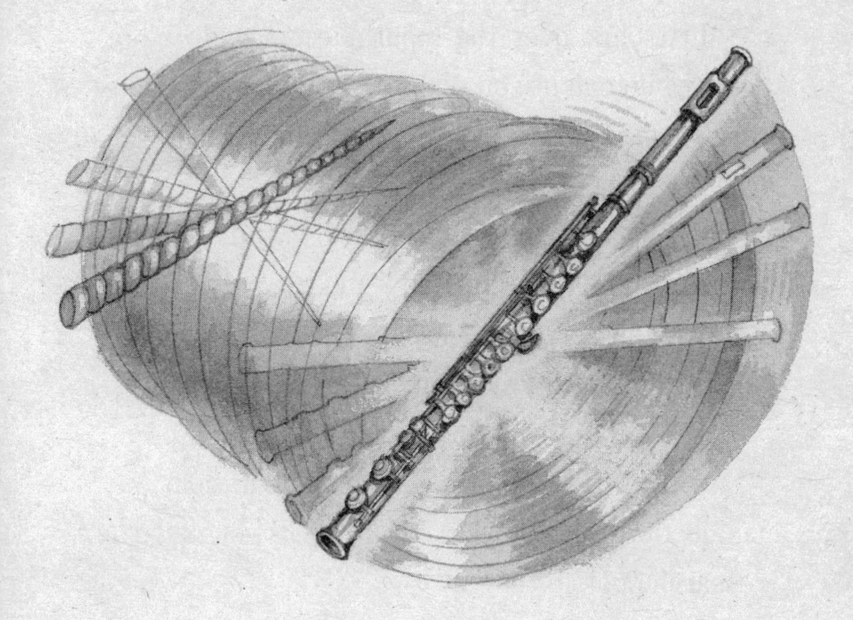

"A flute?" asked Jack.

"A *magic* flute," said Teddy. "Playing this flute will deliver you from danger."

"But Jack and I don't know *how* to play the flute," said Annie.

"Do not worry," said Kathleen. "If the time is right, the flute will make its own music."

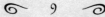

"Just blow over the mouthpiece," said Teddy. "And while one of you plays, the other must make up a song. Whatever you sing will come true."

"Cool!" said Annie.

"But when your song has ended, the flute's magic will end, too," said Kathleen. "You can only use the flute's magic once, so choose the time wisely."

"Okay, got it!" said Annie.

"Are you ready to go?" asked Kathleen.

"Uh, wait," said Jack. "Party invitation . . . magic flute . . . Is that all? Don't you have a research book for us?"

"On this journey, Merlin wants you to rely only on your wits and your talents," said Teddy.

"Oh. Okay," said Jack, though he wasn't sure he had many talents.

"Tell the magic tree house where to go by pointing to the words on the invitation," said Kathleen.

Annie pointed to the words *Summer Palace.* But before she made her wish, she looked at Teddy and Kathleen. "I hope we see you again very soon," she said. "Say hi to Merlin and Morgan when you go back to Camelot."

"And Penny, too," said Jack.

Kathleen and Teddy both smiled.

"Yes, we will," said Teddy.

Annie took a deep breath. "Okay. I wish we could go *there*!" she said. "To the summer palace!"

The wind started to blow.

The tree house started to spin.

It spun faster and faster.

Then everything was still.

Absolutely still.

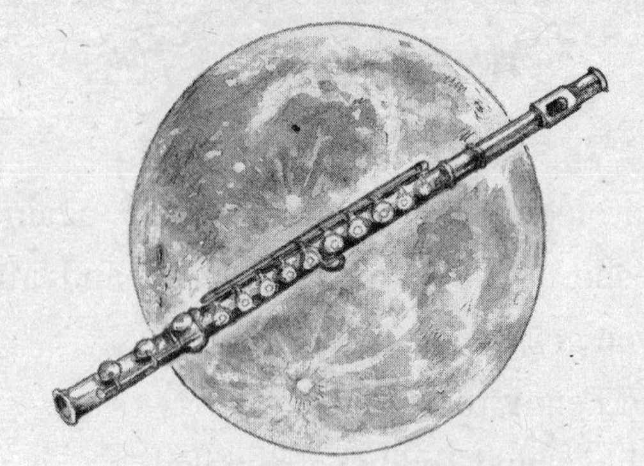

CHAPTER TWO

Put On Your Wig!

Jack opened his eyes. He looked down at his clothes. He was wearing a blue velvet coat, a long vest, and knee-length pants. His shoes were black with shiny buckles.

Jack looked up at Annie and burst out laughing. Her pigtails had changed into thick, cigar-shaped curls. She was wearing a pink dress covered with lace and bows. There was a big hoop underneath her skirt to hold it out. The hoop, the skirt, and lots of petticoats were all bunched up around Annie.

"You look like you're standing in a basket," said Jack.

"*You* look like an old woman," said Annie. She pointed at Jack's head.

Jack reached up and lifted off a black velvet hat. But something else was on his head, too. He pulled off a white wig with curls on the side and a ponytail in the back.

"A *wig*?" said Jack. His nose tickled. He sneezed, and a cloud of white powder puffed from his wig. "It's covered in powder! I can't wear this!"

"Yes, you can," said Annie. "If I have to wear *this*"—she shook her dress—"you have to wear *that*."

"But why are we dressed this way?" asked Jack.

"Because we're going to a fancy party in a palace a long time ago," said Annie.

"Okay, but where's the palace?" said Jack.

Jack and Annie went to the window and looked out. They had landed in a row of trees that lined a

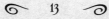

cobblestone street. At the far end of the street, glittering horse-drawn coaches were parked outside tall iron gates.

"I wonder if the palace is beyond those gates," said Annie, pointing.

“I don’t know,” said Jack. “I wish we had a research book to help us.”

“Merlin wants us to rely on our wits and talents,” said Annie.

“Yeah,” said Jack, “whatever that means.”

Bells rang in the distance: *bong, bong, bong, bong, bong.*

"Five bongs," said Annie. "What time's the party?"

Jack looked at their invitation and read aloud, "'Five o'clock in the evening.'"

"Oh, no! We're going to be late!" said Annie. "Put on your wig!"

Jack crammed his wig back onto his head and put on his hat. He pushed the silver flute and invitation into a deep pocket in his coat.

Annie squashed her hoopskirt and squeezed through the opening in the tree house floor. "It's hard to climb down a rope ladder in this dress!" she said.

"Be careful! Go slow!" said Jack.

"But we have to hurry!" said Annie. She jumped off the ladder and landed on the ground.

Jack hurried down the ladder. "You okay?" he asked.

"I'm fine," said Annie, standing up. "Just got a

little dirty." She brushed off her dress. "Let's ask one of those guys about the palace." She pointed toward the coach drivers outside the iron gates. "Hurry!"

Annie started to run. Her skirt swung wildly from side to side like a giant bell.

"Slow down!" said Jack, rushing to catch up with her. "You can't run in that big skirt—you look ridiculous. Besides, we need to discuss our mission before we go to this party."

"It's simple," said Annie. "We're looking for a brilliant—"

"I know—artist," finished Jack. "But how do we find this person?"

"We'll get to that part soon enough," said Annie. "First let's find the party."

Jack and Annie walked toward the fancy coaches parked near the gates. "Where's our invitation?" asked Annie.

"Here." Jack pulled the invitation out of his pocket.

"Excuse me," said Annie, walking up to the driver of a golden coach pulled by two white horses. "We're looking for the summer palace." Jack showed their invitation to the man.

The driver nodded approvingly. "Ah, so you are guests of the imperial family!" he said. "But why are you arriving on foot? Where is your coach?"

"Um, our driver let us out back there," said Annie, pointing down the street.

"I fear he let you out too soon," said the driver. "You still have quite a distance to go."

"We do?" said Annie.

"Yes," said the driver. "I have already delivered my employer and his family to the palace. I was waiting here until the party ended. But if you like, I can take you there. Young nobles should always arrive by coach."

"Oh, thanks!" said Annie.

Jack straightened his shoulders and tried to look noble.

"My name is Josef," said the man. "Come, let

me help you up." Josef held out his hand. Annie took it, and Josef helped her up onto a cushioned leather seat.

Josef helped Jack up, too. Then the friendly driver climbed onto a bench behind the milk white horses.

"Wow, I feel like Cinderella going to the ball," Annie said to Jack.

Josef snapped the reins. The horses took off, and the guards opened the gates. The coach clattered over the cobblestones into an immense square.

The square was bathed in the last light of day. Monks in brown robes strolled around a huge fountain. Soldiers in uniforms rode on horseback. On the far side of the square was a long building. It had bright yellow walls and dozens of windows that flashed with the light of the setting sun.

"Is *that* the summer palace, sir?" Annie called to Josef.

"Yes, indeed," Josef said over his shoulder.

"And there is much more that you cannot see! Behind the palace is a garden of nearly three hundred acres. It has beautiful flowers, orchards, fountains, and a zoo."

"A zoo?" said Jack.

"Hello, boy and girl!" came a high little voice. A closed blue coach passed them. A small boy wearing a white wig was calling from a window. He pointed at Jack and laughed. "Your wig is crooked!" he shouted in his high voice.

Before the boy could say more, someone pulled him back from the window, and the blue coach rumbled away.

"What an annoying kid," said Jack. "*Is* my wig crooked?"

"A little." Annie lifted Jack's hat off. She tried to straighten his wig as they lurched and swayed on the cushioned seat. "There," she said. "That's better."

Josef drove the horses to the front of the palace. The coach stopped near a staircase that led up to a terrace. Josef helped Jack and Annie down from their seat.

"I can tell this is your first visit to the palace," said Josef. "At the door, you must show the guard in the red uniform your invitation. He will direct you to the receiving line."

"The receiving line? What's that?" said Jack.

"That is where you will wait to be introduced," said Josef.

"Introduced to who?" asked Jack.

"To Her Imperial Majesty Maria Theresa. She is Archduchess of Austria; Queen of Hungary, Croatia, and Bohemia; and Empress of the Holy Roman Empire," said Josef.

"Oh, right," said Annie.

Yeah, right, thought Jack. *Help!*

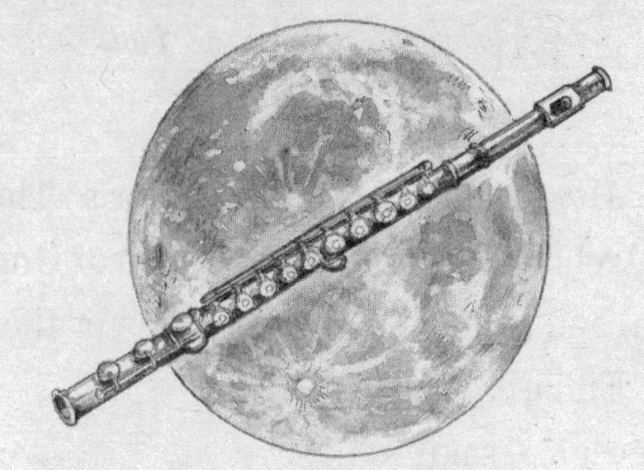

CHAPTER THREE

Her Imperial Majesty

"Thanks for your help, Josef," said Annie.

"Yeah, thanks a lot," said Jack.

"You're very welcome," said Josef. "I hope you will enjoy yourselves at the party."

"We will," said Annie. "Bye."

As the coachman climbed back into his carriage, Annie turned to Jack. "This is so cool!" she said.

Not really, thought Jack. He didn't know how he was supposed to act with Her Imperial Majesty whatever-the-rest-of-her-name-was! His hands felt clammy. "What do we do when we meet her? What do we say?" he asked.

"We just watch what other people do," said Annie, "and we copy them. Come on."

Jack and Annie walked over to the sweeping stairway. They started up the steps, following the other party guests. The women all wore glittering jewels and gowns with giant hoopskirts. The men wore wigs with white curls flowing down over the collars of their long coats. All the clothes were made of silk and satin and velvet in rich colors and patterns.

"Oh, brother," said Jack.

"What?" said Annie.

"There's that kid who yelled at me," Jack said.

The small boy from the blue coach was standing at the top of the stairs. He wore a lilac-colored coat with gold braid. A tiny sword hung from his side.

"A sword?" said Jack. "That's ridiculous. He can't be more than four or five years old."

The boy turned and caught sight of Jack and Annie. A big smile crossed his round face. He waved at them.

"He's cute," said Annie. She waved back.

"Not really," said Jack.

A man grabbed the boy's hand and pulled him into the palace.

"And he thought *I* looked funny," said Jack. "How's my wig now?"

Annie giggled. "It's crooked again," she said. "And your ears are poking out. Hold on."

Jack and Annie stopped on the stairs. Annie grabbed both sides of Jack's wig and gave it a good yank.

"Move along, children. You're holding up the line!" a woman behind them said.

Annie picked up her hoopskirt, and she and Jack hurried up the stairs. At the top, Jack pulled their invitation out of his pocket again. He led Annie into the palace and showed the invitation to a guard in a red uniform.

"Follow the line through the lantern room and into the Great Rosa Room," the guard said.

Jack saw a line of party guests walking slowly through a candlelit room. He and Annie quickly joined the line. The room was filled with sounds of whispering and the rustling of silk.

A young girl in a white dress with red roses was standing near Jack and Annie. When the line moved, Jack waited for the girl to go ahead.

The girl smiled. "I'm not in line," she said in a soft voice. "I'm waiting for my brother."

Jack nodded, and he and Annie stepped forward. Jack craned his neck to get a better view inside the Great Rosa Room. He couldn't see Her Imperial Majesty yet, but he could see part of the fancy room with its red velvet chairs and gold-trimmed, glossy white walls.

Another guest entered the Great Rosa Room, and Jack and Annie took a step closer to the door. *Now* Jack could see Her Imperial Majesty. She was a tall, plump woman dressed in a blue silk gown with ruffles. To Jack's surprise, the little kid with the sword was sitting on her lap! A long row of older children stood behind her.

Jack turned to Annie. "Who do you think those kids are?" he asked.

Annie shrugged.

"They are the children of Her Imperial Majesty," said the girl who had spoken to Jack earlier. "The imperial children."

"Thanks," said Annie.

"The imperial children look pretty unfriendly," Jack whispered to Annie. The little boy with the sword was the only one smiling.

"Well, it must be really hard to just stand there wearing stiff clothes and wigs while people are being received," Annie whispered back.

"Prepare yourselves. You are next," a servant at the door said to Jack and Annie.

Oh, no! thought Jack. He'd been too busy looking at the imperial children to watch the guests in front of him. "What do we do when we meet

Her Imperial Majesty?" he asked Annie frantically.

"I don't know! I forgot to watch!" she said. Annie turned to the girl in the white dress. "Um—excuse me? Can you tell us what to do when we meet Her Imperial Majesty?" she asked.

The girl leaned close to Annie and whispered, "Enter the room and announce your names. Then walk to the middle of the room. You must curtsy; he must bow. Next go directly up to Her Imperial Majesty and do the same."

"Got it," said Annie.

"Oh, and remember—" the girl said to Jack, "do not rise from the second bow until Her Imperial Majesty tells you to. Do not even look up. Rise only when she says 'rise.' Then step backward out of the room."

"Backward?" said Jack.

"Yes. You must never turn your back on Her Imperial Majesty," said the girl. "It would be considered very bad manners."

"Thanks!" said Jack. He was grateful to the

girl for giving them such important information.

The servant at the door turned and nodded to Jack and Annie. The two of them stepped into the Great Rosa Room.

"Annie of Frog Creek!" Annie said loudly.

"Jack, also of Frog Creek!" said Jack.

Jack and Annie walked slowly to the center of the room; Her Imperial Majesty and the imperial children watched them closely. The little boy with the sword waved at them. Annie curtsied and Jack gave a low bow.

Then Jack and Annie walked closer to Her Imperial Majesty. She had a double chin, a high forehead, and lots of teeny blond curls. Jack smiled at her, but her pale face stayed very serious.

Annie curtsied again, and Jack gave a second bow. As he bowed, he remembered that it was bad manners to rise or look up before Her Imperial Majesty told him to.

Jack stared at the shiny buckles on his shoes, waiting to hear Her Imperial Majesty say "rise."

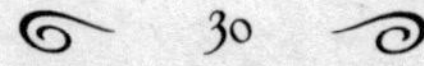

Maybe I'm not bowing low enough, Jack thought. He bent over a few inches more. To his horror, the silver flute slipped out of his coat pocket! It clattered to the floor. As Jack grabbed it, his hat fell off.

The imperial children snickered.

Clutching the flute, Jack reached for his hat with his other hand. But when he grabbed his hat, his wig fell off! Jack reached for his wig, but powder got in his nose, and he sneezed. As he sneezed, he slipped on the polished floor and fell to his knees. Gripping his wig, his hat, and his flute, Jack scrambled back up to his bowing position. But he still hadn't heard Her Imperial Majesty tell him to rise!

The imperial children laughed loudly. Jack even heard Her Imperial Majesty laughing! *She probably can't speak because she's laughing so hard,* thought Jack. He didn't know what to do. His face was burning hot. *You've got to get out of here!* he told himself.

Still bowing, Jack began backing up with little steps—until he bumped into a wall.

As the imperial children howled with laughter, Jack turned his head and saw Annie peeking out from a doorway, giggling. He backed over to her.

Annie grabbed his coattails and pulled him out of the Great Rosa Room.

The imperial children clapped and cheered. Jack heard one of the girls say between gulps of laughter, “Who was that fool?”

“That was Jack of Frog Creek!” answered the small boy in his high voice. And they all laughed loudly again.

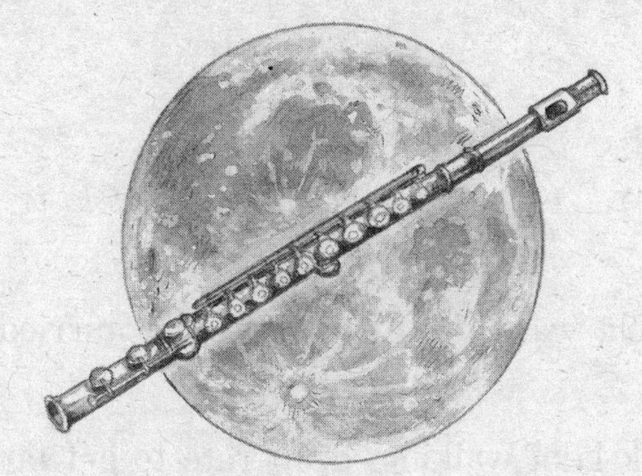

CHAPTER FOUR

Jack of Frog Creek!

Annie was laughing so hard that she could barely stand up. "What—what happened to you in there?" she said. "After I curtsied, I left. When I looked back in the room, you were still bowing!"

"She didn't say 'rise'!" said Jack.

"Yes, she did, dummy!" said Annie.

"Well, I didn't hear her!" said Jack. He turned away from Annie and started walking as fast as he could. He strode through one elegant room into another. He didn't know where he was. *These rooms all look the same,* he thought angrily, *with*

stupid velvet furniture and stupid gold-trimmed walls.

"Jack, wait!" Annie called. She hurried after him.

Jack kept walking, desperate to get far away from the scene of his disaster. Finally he came to a door that led outside. He opened it and stepped out onto a long marble terrace overlooking the back of the palace. Bright silvery light from a full moon shone on a huge garden.

Jack stood in the chilly air, trying to calm down. He took a deep breath. He desperately wanted to run back to the tree house and go home.

"Jack!" Annie slipped out to join him. "I'm sorry I called you a dummy," she said. "Are you okay?"

"I didn't hear her say to rise," said Jack. "And the flute fell out of my coat and my hat came off . . . and my wig . . . and I sneezed and I slipped. . . . Come on, let's leave. We can go down these stairs."

"No, we can't leave now," said Annie. "We have

a mission from Merlin. Don't feel bad. Hardly anyone saw what you did."

"Yeah, except Her Imperial Majesty and all those imperial kids," said Jack. "They all laughed at me."

"They weren't being mean," said Annie. "You were funny. Here, give me your wig."

Jack handed Annie his wig, and she put it back on his head and straightened it.

"Your hat," she said.

Jack gave her his hat, and she placed it over his wig. "Hide the flute," said Annie.

Jack stuck the silver flute back into his pocket. "I don't know what we need this flute for," he said. "There's nothing dangerous here. I don't get this whole mission."

"We'll figure it out. Let's just go back in," said Annie. She pulled Jack back inside the palace.

"So what do we do now?" asked Jack.

"We should find the party we were invited to," said Annie. "That must be what Merlin wanted us to do." She pointed across the room. People were streaming through a set of doors into another room. Loud party noises came from inside: the chatter of guests, tinkling china, and harp and violin music.

Jack pulled back. But Annie took him by the arm. "Don't worry, I'll bet there are hundreds of people in there," she said. "We'll get lost in the crowd."

"But what about all those kids and Her Imperial Majesty?" Jack asked.

"They don't care about us," said Annie. "They have too many other guests to think about. Come on." Annie led Jack through the double doors into the party room.

"Whoa," breathed Jack. He and Annie stopped and stared.

The party room was the size of a football field. Grand paintings covered the towering ceiling. Everything was trimmed in gold. The glossy white walls and tall mirrors reflected the glow of at least a thousand candles.

Musicians played harps and violins while hundreds of guests stood around long dinner tables, chatting and laughing. Women fanned themselves, their diamonds and rubies flashing in the candlelight. The air smelled of perfume, powder, and roses.

"Okay! Let's talk about our mission," said Annie. "We have to help a brilliant artist get on the right path to bring joy to the world."

"Yeah, but first we have to find one . . . ," said Jack.

"Right, so let's look around," said Annie.

Jack and Annie started drifting together through the huge room. Jack gazed at the grown-ups. Dressed in their finery, they all looked pretty much the same. *What does a brilliant artist look like?* Jack wondered.

"Jack of Frog Creek!" came a high little voice.

Oh, no! thought Jack. He whirled around.

The boy with the tiny sword was grinning up at him. "I have been looking all over for you!" he said.

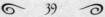

"Hi!" said Annie. "What's your name?"

"Wolfie," said the boy.

"That's a funny name," said Annie.

"So is Jack of Frog Creek!" said Wolfie. His eyes shone as he looked up at Jack. "Are you a clown?" he asked.

Annie giggled.

"Yeah, that's right, I'm a clown," said Jack.

"How old are you, Wolfie?" said Annie, changing the subject.

"Six!" the little boy said.

"Six?" said Jack. This kid looked more like a four-year-old, he thought, five at the most.

"And I'm eleven," a girl said.

For the first time, Jack noticed the girl standing behind Wolfie. She wore a white dress with red roses. She was the girl who had helped them in line!

"Hi!" said Annie.

"Hello again," the girl said in a soft, lovely voice. "I am Wolfie's sister."

Jack felt his face grow red. The girl must have seen him make a fool of himself.

"My name is Nannerl," said the girl.

"Nan-nerl?" said Annie, trying to pronounce her name.

The girl smiled. "You can call me Nan if you like," she said. "Wolfie and I enjoyed your performance in the Great Rosa Room, Jack. You must be very proud. Her Imperial Majesty does not laugh easily."

Jack shrugged and scratched his wig. He wondered if the girl was joking. But she looked serious, so he decided not to tell her he hadn't *meant* to be funny.

"Do you call your mother 'Her Imperial Majesty'?" Annie asked Nan.

Nan looked confused. "No."

"We call her Mama!" said Wolfie.

"But you just said Her Imperial Majesty doesn't laugh much," said Annie.

"Oh, Her Imperial Majesty is not our mother!" Nan said. "Our mother is back home in Salzburg. We are just visiting the palace."

"Then why was Wolfie sitting on Her Imperial Majesty's lap?" asked Annie.

"Because she likes me very much!" Wolfie piped up.

Oh, brother, thought Jack.

"Wolfie, be modest," said Nan, shaking her head. "Actually, Wolfie jumped in her lap when we presented ourselves. I tried to grab him, but Her Imperial Majesty wanted him to stay with her."

"Were all those other kids imperial children?" Annie asked.

"Oh, yes," said Nan. "Papa taught me all their names before we came here: Leopold, Ferdinand, Maximilian, Joseph, Maria Antonia, Maria Caroline, Maria Josepha, Maria Amalie, Maria Elisabeth, Maria Christina, Maria Johanna, and Maria Anna."

"Hmm," said Jack. "Maria's a popular name around here."

Nan laughed. Jack liked making her laugh.

"Hey, look at me!" said Wolfie. He pulled off his wig. He pretended to sneeze and then fell to the floor. "I'm Jack the Clown!" he said.

"Ha-ha. Very funny," said Jack, forcing a smile.

He'd had just about enough of Wolfie.

"Nan, we have a question for you," said Annie. "Do you know if there are any brilliant artists here at the party?"

"I haven't really been in Vienna long enough to meet many people," said Nan. "But Papa told me that artists do live—"

"Wait!" Wolfie broke in. He jumped to his feet. "I know someone here who is *very* brilliant."

"Who?" asked Annie.

"Me!" said Wolfie. And he bowed.

"Wolfie," said Nan, shaking her head.

"Right," said Jack. He turned back to Nan. "What were you about to say?"

But Wolfie broke in again. "Nan and I are *both* brilliant!" he exclaimed in his high voice. "Our papa teaches us math, history, writing, reading, geography, music, drawing, riding, fencing, and dancing." Wolfie raised his arms over his head and did a little dance step.

Annie laughed.

"Wolfie, stop!" said Nan.

Yeah, cool it, kid, thought Jack.

"Do you want to go outside and play in the garden?" Wolfie asked Jack and Annie. "We can *all* dance!"

"I don't think so, Wolfie," said Jack. "But thanks." He turned back to Nan. "So! What were you going to tell us about artists?"

"Oh, yes," said Nan. "Papa told me that Her Imperial Majesty often invites artists to live in the palace and work here."

"Perfect!" said Jack.

"Do you think any of them are here at the party now?" asked Annie.

"I don't know," said Nan. "The palace is very big. Papa told us that more than fifteen hundred people live here. Why are you looking for brilliant artists?"

"Oh," said Annie, "we're on a mission to—"

Jack interrupted her. ". . . to party with brilliant artists," he finished. "That's our mission."

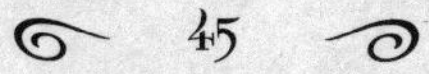

Then he laughed because he knew he sounded stupid.

Nan laughed, too. "I see," she said. "All right then, at dinner I will ask Papa where the artists stay."

"Thank you!" said Jack. *Finally,* he thought, they were starting their Merlin mission!

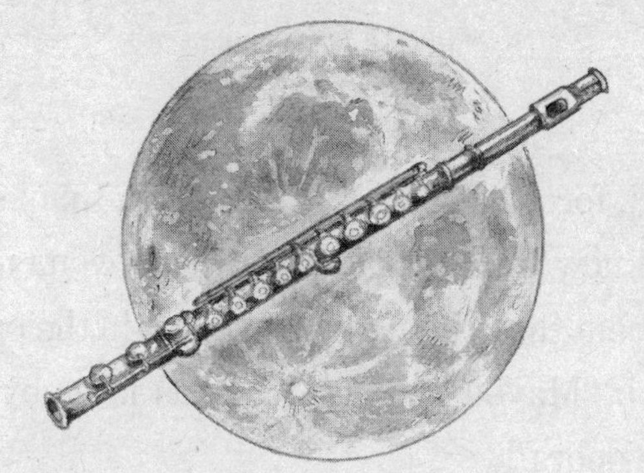

CHAPTER FIVE

Bad Manners

A servant rang a bell. Other servants began carrying in large silver bowls, platters, and trays.

"It is time for dinner now," said Nan. "We must go, Wolfie. We have to find Papa." She helped her little brother put his wig back on.

"But I want to stay with Jack and Annie," whined Wolfie. "I want to play with them in the garden."

"Not now," said Nan. She grabbed Wolfie's hand. "It was nice to talk to you," she said to Jack and Annie. "And I hope we can see you perform again someday, Jack."

Jack forced a smile. "Uh . . . yeah, thanks. Hey, let us know what your dad—I mean, your *papa*—says about the brilliant artists living in the palace," he said. "Maybe you can meet us later by those double doors?"

"Yes, after dinner, we will meet you," said Nan.

"And then we will play in the garden!" said Wolfie.

"No, you and I will have other things to do, Wolfie, remember?" said Nan. "Come along now." She pulled her little brother away.

"But I want to play with Jack the Clown!" Wolfie wailed.

Jack and Annie watched Wolfie and Nan disappear into the crowd.

"I am *not* a clown," Jack said darkly.

"Don't worry about him," said Annie. "He really admires you."

"Lucky me," said Jack.

The bell sounded again. People started moving toward the dinner tables.

"Where should we sit?" said Annie.

"Anywhere," said Jack, "as long as we're out of the way." He still wanted to hide from the imperial children. "What about that table at the end of the room? Near the door?"

"Sure."

Jack led the way to the table at the far end of the room. "Let's grab seats while we can," he said to Annie.

As grown-ups hovered near the table talking and laughing, Jack and Annie sat down in two chairs. Steaming platters of food lined the middle of the table: beef stew, mashed potatoes, sausages, dumplings, cabbage, spiced apples, and gingerbread.

Jack's mouth watered. He hadn't realized how hungry he was. "Okay, here's our plan," he said to Annie. "We'll eat first. Then Nan will tell us where all the artists live, and we'll get to work."

"Excuse me, young man and young lady," someone said in a snippy tone.

Jack and Annie turned around in their chairs. An elderly couple stood glaring at them.

"The empress herself designed the seating plan," the man said. "And I can assure you these are *not* your seats."

"Furthermore," said the woman, "*no one* sits until Her Imperial Majesty is seated."

Jack and Annie jumped up from their chairs.

"Oops!" said Annie.

"Sorry!" said Jack.

"Our mistake," said Annie. "Excuse us."

Jack and Annie walked away from the table. "That was bad manners," Annie said to Jack.

"Who, us or them?" said Jack.

"Us," Annie said. "I wonder where *our* seats are."

"I have a feeling we're not a part of the empress's seating plan," said Jack. His face felt hot again. His wig itched like crazy.

Suddenly a hush fell over the room. The harp and violin music stopped. Everyone stopped talking.

Her Imperial Majesty had entered through the main doors. The imperial children followed her. Her Majesty led them to the table in the middle of the room. Everyone else stood silently, waiting for the imperial family to sit down.

"We have to get out of here *now*," Jack whispered to Annie. "Soon we'll be the only ones left standing."

"Like musical chairs," said Annie.

"Right," said Jack. "Forget dinner. Let's go look for where the artists are staying. We can't wait for Nan to ask her dad."

As all the guests sat down, Jack and Annie hurried toward the door.

"Jack the Clown!" came a high voice.

Jack looked over his shoulder. Wolfie was waving from one of the tables.

Annie waved back.

"Don't wave! Keep going," said Jack. He grabbed Annie's hand and pulled her out of the party room. They hurried into yet another elegant room with red velvet furniture and gold-trimmed walls.

"Keep going," said Jack. He led the way into another fancy room.

"Jack and Annie, wait!" came a cry.

"I hear Wolfie!" said Annie.

"Darn!" Jack quickly closed the door behind them. "Keep moving!" he said.

"We can't," said Annie. "That's mean. We should wait for him."

"But he'll slow down our mission!" said Jack. "When are we going to get started?"

"Calm down," said Annie. "We'll just tell him we can't hang out with him now because we have something important that we have to do."

Jack heaved a sigh. "Okay."

"Jack! Annie!"

Jack opened the door.

Wolfie ran right into him. "There you are!" the little boy said, smiling. "I was looking for you!"

"No kidding," said Jack.

"Yes!" Wolfie said. "Are you leaving?"

"Not yet, we have to do something important," said Jack. "And you can't come with us."

Wolfie's smile vanished.

"Sorry," said Jack.

"But I want you to come to the garden with me," said Wolfie.

"Not now," said Jack. "Wolfie, listen to me. Listen carefully. Annie and I have to do something really, really important. And we have to do it all by ourselves."

Wolfie's bottom lip started to quiver. *Oh, no,* thought Jack. *He's going to cry.*

A tear ran down the little boy's cheek.

"Aww, Wolfie, don't cry," Annie said gently.

"Wolfie! Wolfie!" someone called. Nan burst into the room. "Wolfie, what are you doing? Papa is very upset!"

"I want to play with Jack and Annie," said Wolfie. Another big tear ran down his cheek.

"Please, Wolfie," Nan begged. "You know you

have a big responsibility tonight. You have to—"

"No!" wailed Wolfie, stamping his foot. "No, no, no! I never get to play!"

"Wolfie, stop!" said Nan. "Please do not be this way. Not now, of all times! You will kill Papa!"

"Wolfie! Wolfie!" came a deep voice.

"He's in here, Papa!" Nan called. "Come, Wolfie." She took Wolfie's hand, but he pulled away from her.

"No! I want to play!" shouted Wolfie. And he charged out of the room.

"Wolfie?" A portly man in a wig burst through another door. "Where is he? Where is my son?"

"Oh, Papa!" said Nan. "Wolfie ran away!"

"Ran away?" The man threw his hands in the air. "We must find him!" he cried.

"Papa, calm down!" said Nan.

"We will fail utterly without him!" cried her papa. And he rushed out of the room.

"Papa! Papa!" yelled Nan. And she hurried after her father.

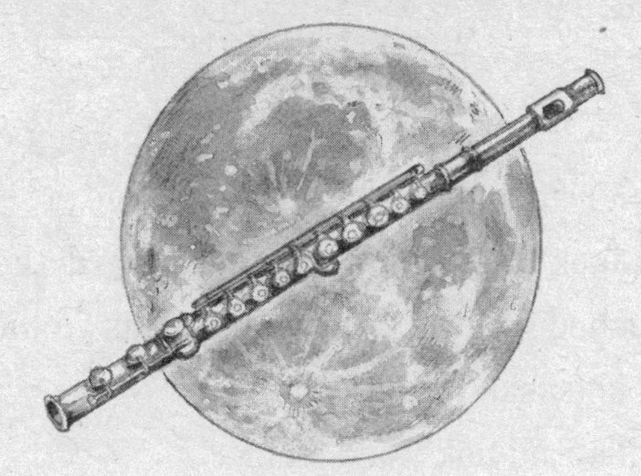

CHAPTER SIX

Under the Moon

"Good grief," breathed Jack. "That family has problems."

"Maybe we should help them," said Annie.

"No, we can't," said Jack. "Right now we have our *own* problem. We have to start working on our mission. Darn! I should have asked Nan's dad about the artists in the palace."

"I think he's too upset to think about that now," said Annie.

"You're right," said Jack. "So we need to find some friendly people who work here and ask them."

"Let's go look for help," said Annie.

As Jack and Annie started toward the door, Nan rushed into the room again. "Has Wolfie come back?" she asked frantically.

"I'm afraid not," said Annie.

"Oh, dear! Papa will die if Wolfie doesn't return soon!" said Nan, near tears. "Can you help me find him, please?"

"Well, we'd *really* like to," said Jack, "but—"

"Please!" said Nan again. "Please?"

Jack sighed. "Okay," he said. "Sure."

"Thank you!" said Nan. "The palace is very large. I'll go this way, and you go that way. Surely one of us will find him!" She hurried out of the room.

"I'll bet I know where Wolfie is," said Annie. "The garden. Remember he kept talking about the garden?"

"Oh, yeah. I think the garden is below that terrace where I went after everyone laughed at me," said Jack. "Let's go check."

Jack led Annie back through one of the elegant

palace rooms and into the party room. Everyone was still seated, eating dinner and talking loudly. No one noticed as Jack and Annie hurried through the double doors and slipped into the room off the terrace.

Jack opened the door, and he and Annie stepped outside. The air was chilly, but it felt good. Jack pulled off his hat and his wig. He gave his head a good scratch.

Annie looked down at the moonlit garden. "Do you think that's the garden Wolfie was talking about?" she said.

The silver light of the full moon shone on a large square with flower beds and fountains. Woods bordered the square. Cricket sounds filled the night.

"Probably," said Jack. "Wolfie!"

There was no answer.

"Let's go down and look for him," said Annie.

Leaving his wig and hat behind, Jack followed Annie down the stone stairway. As they started across the square, a strange sound came from the woods: *AI-YEE!*

"What was *that*?" said Jack.

Two creatures scampered out from the trees.

"Ahh!" said Jack.

"Don't worry," said Annie. "It's just a squirrel and a cat."

The squirrel dashed over the flower beds and disappeared. The cat ran after it.

"Yeah, but what was that noise from the woods?" said Jack. "I've never heard a squirrel or a cat make a sound like that."

Another sound came from behind the trees: *WHOOP-WHOOP-WHOOP!*

"What was *that*?" Jack said.

"An owl maybe?" said Annie.

"I've never heard an owl make a noise like that!" said Jack. "Have you?"

KER-LOO! KER-LOO!

"Yikes! What was *that*?" said Annie.

"I don't know. Those woods sound like a jungle," said Jack.

"Wolfie!" yelled Annie.

There was no answer. Wind shook the treetops. The cricket chirps grew louder.

"This place feels really weird. Let's go back inside," said Jack. "I don't think Wolfie's out here."

"Wait a minute," said Annie. "I think I just heard him."

Jack and Annie both listened. A faint little cry came from the woods. "Annie! Jack!"

"Wolfie *is* out there!" said Annie. "Wolfie!" She picked up her hoopskirt. She hurried across the square and disappeared down a path that led into the woods.

"Annie, wait!" Jack called. He started after her, but then—

WHOOP-WHOOP-WHOOP!

Jack froze. He was *sure* the whooping sound wasn't coming from an owl.

EEE-EEE!

Was that Annie screaming? Jack wondered. "Annie?" he yelled. He dashed across the moonlit garden and ran down the path to the woods. He stopped between the trees. "Annie?" he called again.

EEE-EEE! Something leapt down from a tree branch and landed on the path. "Ahhh!" said Jack, jumping back. It looked like a baboon! *EEE-EEE!* The baboon bounded away!

KER-LOO! KER-LOO! Jack looked up. Overhead a huge crane glided through the air. *KER-LOO! KER-LOO!*

AI-YEE! A crowned peacock stood in the moonlight, fanning its green and gold tail feathers.

What's going on? Jack thought. *This is crazy!*

AI-YEE! the peacock cried again.

Jack heard a rustling in the bushes. Something was moving through the woods, grunting, snorting, and growling. A huge bear lumbered onto the moonlit path! Standing on its hind legs, the bear looked about ten feet tall. It growled.

"Hi?" Jack croaked.

The bear growled again. It stepped toward Jack, raking the air with its huge claws.

Jack began backing away. Then he turned and ran as fast as he could. As he wound his way between the trees, he could hear the bear crashing through the woods behind him.

WHOOP-WHOOP-WHOOP!

A dog-like animal bounded across Jack's path. Jack recognized it. It was a laughing hyena—a creature he and Annie had seen on the plains of Africa! *What's going on?* Jack wondered again. *Where are these animals coming from?*

"Jack!" yelled Annie. "Over here!"

Annie was hiding behind a tree. Jack ran over and crouched beside her. He could hear the bear growling and thrashing through the brush.

"A huge bear's chasing me!" Jack said.

"I know! He was chasing me, too!" said Annie.

"I saw a baboon, a hyena, and a crane!" sputtered Jack. "What's happening?"

"I don't know!" whispered Annie. "Look!"

From behind the tree, they watched an ostrich prance through the moonlight. Behind the ostrich, a gazelle stepped softly over the path in the woods, looking from side to side. Then the peacock strutted back into sight, fanning its luminous feathers.

"It's like a zoo in these woods," said Jack.

"Oh, wow, that's *it*!" said Annie.

"What do you mean?" said Jack.

"The *zoo*! That's where they're from!" said Annie. "Remember our coach driver said the palace had a zoo!"

"But zoos have cages!" said Jack. "The animals don't just roam around free!"

"Jack! Annie!" Wolfie's voice was close by.

"That's Wolfie again!" said Annie. "Oh, wow. I'll bet *Wolfie* let the animals out of their cages."

"Help!" Wolfie called.

"Oh, man, that kid's crazy," said Jack.

"I know, but we have to help him!" said Annie.

Annie picked up her skirt. She and Jack crept from their hiding place and walked cautiously down the path.

"Jack! Annie! Help me!"

Jack and Annie kept going, stepping in and out of the shadowy moonlight. Suddenly Annie gasped and pointed. Wolfie was sitting in the crook of a tree up ahead.

A large spotted animal was crouched below him.

"A leopard!" whispered Jack.

The leopard looked up at Wolfie and growled.

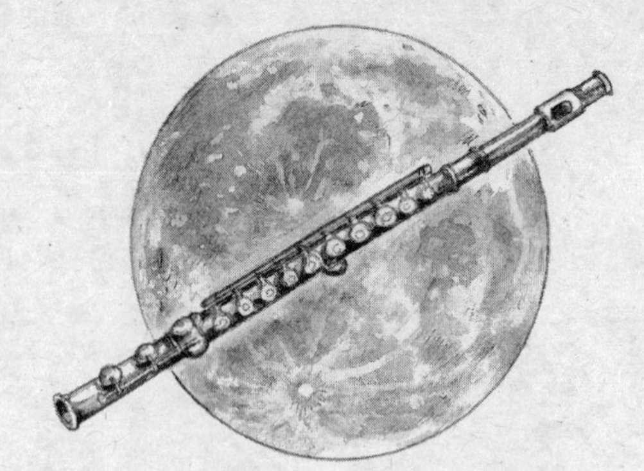

CHAPTER SEVEN

Follow Me

"Stand back!" Wolfie shouted at the leopard. "I have a sword! And I'm not afraid to use it!"

"Oh, brother," whispered Jack. There was no way Wolfie's tiny sword could ward off the huge leopard. But if Jack and Annie rushed in to rescue Wolfie, the leopard might leap up and attack him.

Annie nudged Jack's arm. She pointed at the pocket of his coat. She held up her hands, pretending to play a flute.

Jack had forgotten all about their magic flute! He remembered Teddy's words: *Playing this flute will deliver you from danger.*

But what can the flute do? Jack wondered. *How can it help us?* He reached into his pocket and pulled out the flute anyway.

"You play—just blow over the mouthpiece," whispered Annie. "I'll make up a song. Remember, whatever I sing will come true."

Jack nodded and held up the magic flute. It glistened in the light of the moon. Jack wasn't sure he was holding it right, but he hoped it wouldn't matter. He closed his eyes and blew gently across the mouthpiece.

Music streamed from the silver instrument! The pure sound wafted through the air like a feather on the wind. The melody was simple, yet beautiful.

Annie started singing, making up a song:

Leopard, hey, leopard,
Listen to our sound.

The leopard turned its head and looked at Jack and Annie. It pricked up its spotted ears.

Follow me, follow me,
Follow me and the clown.

Clown? thought Jack. *Is that me?* He didn't love Annie's choice of words, but he didn't have time to worry about it. The leopard rose to its feet and began walking toward Jack and Annie.

Jack was so scared that he almost turned and ran away. But he didn't dare. He knew that as soon as he stopped playing the flute, the magic would end.

Annie tugged on Jack's sleeve, and they started walking slowly down the path, back toward the palace. The leopard padded silently after them as Annie kept singing:

Wolfie, hey, Wolfie,
Jump down, jump down . . .
Follow me, follow me,
Follow me and the clown.

Without a word, Wolfie bravely hopped down from the tree. He followed the leopard, Jack, and

Annie. They all walked down the path between the trees. Jack had no idea where they were going. He only knew that he should keep playing, Annie should keep singing, and they should all keep moving.

Jack heard branches breaking. He heard grunting and snorting. The giant bear lumbered out from behind some trees. But Jack kept playing, and Annie kept singing:

Bear, hey, bear,
No need to frown.
Follow me, follow me,
Follow me and the clown.

The bear followed Jack, Annie, the leopard, and Wolfie down the path. The moonlight grew brighter and brighter. The magic music was making the night as bright as day!

Next the hyena's laugh rippled through the air. *WHOOP-WHOOP!* The hyena slunk out from behind a tree trunk.

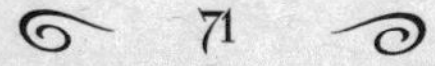

Jack kept playing, and Annie kept singing:

Hyena, hey, hyena,
We're glad you've been found.
Follow me, follow me,
Follow me and the clown.

The hyena joined the parade.

More creatures appeared: the gazelle and the ostrich and the peacock. Annie sang to them as Jack played the magic flute:

Hey, gazelle! Hey, ostrich!
Hey, bird with a crown!
Follow me, follow me,
Follow me and the clown.

The animals all joined the parade. Jack heard Wolfie laughing with joy. He looked back and saw the little boy waving his arms as if he were conducting the magic music, a big grin on his face.

Jack kept playing, and Annie kept singing:

All creatures who fly,
Fly after this tune.

All creatures who walk,
Walk under the moon.
All creatures who crawl,
Crawl over the ground.
Follow me, follow me,
Follow me and the clown.

Baboons and bunnies, snakes and squirrels, lizards and foxes—all the ordinary and extraordinary creatures in the woods followed Jack and Annie. On the other side of the wide square, candles twinkled in the rear windows of the palace. Jack wondered where he should lead all the wild creatures. Where was the zoo? How could he and Annie get the animals back into their cages?

But Annie had *another* idea, as she sang:

To your forests and plains,
Where you're all free to roam,
To your lands near and far,
Go home now, go home . . .
Go home now, go home . . .
Go home now, go home . . .

As Annie sang the last words over and over, the creatures began to vanish into thin air. The leopard, bear, hyena, ostrich, gazelle, peacock, baboon, and crane all disappeared. Soon, the only animals left in the woods were the ones that belonged there.

Annie stopped singing, Jack stopped playing, and Wolfie stopped waving his hands. The bright light faded to silver moonlight, and the cats, squirrels, and bunnies scampered off into the dark. The garden became quiet and peaceful again, except for the chirping of crickets.

"Where did the wild animals go?" asked Wolfie.

"Home," Annie said simply.

Jack put the flute back in his pocket and heaved a sigh. "Good work," he said to Annie. "But did you have to keep calling me a clown?"

Annie giggled. "Sorry, but 'clown' sounds good with so many other words."

"I'm glad they went home," said Wolfie. "I wanted them to be free."

"Listen, Wolfie," said Jack. "Don't ever, *ever* again try to free animals from a zoo. Someone could have gotten hurt!"

"I'm sorry," said Wolfie. "I promise I'll never do it again. But how did you make them follow you?"

"It wasn't us," said Annie. "It was our music."

"Was it magic?" asked Wolfie.

"Yes, as a matter of fact it was," said Annie.

"Music *is* magic," said Wolfie thoughtfully. "I love music."

"Cool," said Jack.

"I *really* love it!" said Wolfie.

"Uh . . . good," said Jack.

"I love it more than anything!" said Wolfie. He whirled around, clapping his hands and dancing for joy.

What a weird kid, thought Jack.

As Wolfie twirled, the palace clock sounded: *bong, bong, bong, bong, bong, bong, bong.*

"Seven," said Annie. "Seven o'clock."

Wolfie stopped twirling and stumbled dizzily.

"Oh, no! I must go!" he cried. "I will be late!" Wolfie grabbed Jack and Annie. "Come with me! You have to come with me!"

"Uh, okay," said Jack. *Why is Wolfie so frantic?* he wondered.

Wolfie pulled Jack and Annie toward the palace. "Hurry! I cannot be late!" he cried.

"Late for what?" said Jack.

Before Wolfie could answer, someone called his name. "Wolfie! Where are you?" It was Nan. She was standing on the back terrace of the palace. "Wolfie!" she called again.

"Coming!" shouted Wolfie. "Poor Nan! She is waiting for me! Papa is waiting for me! The *whole world* is waiting for me!"

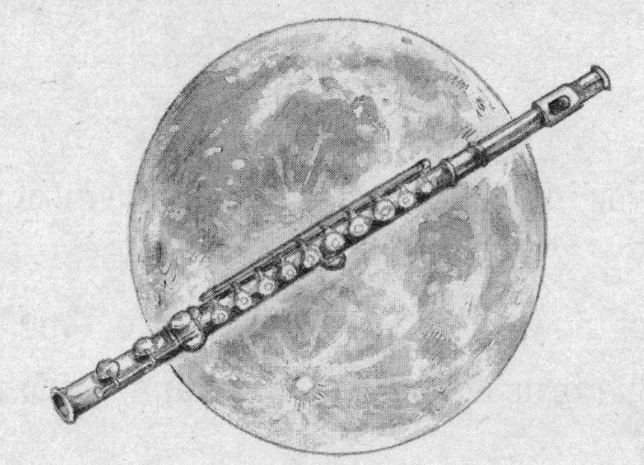

CHAPTER EIGHT

The Hall of Mirrors

Wolfie took off running toward the palace.

"The whole world?" Jack said to Annie. "I don't think so."

Annie smiled. "Come on, let's go back inside," she said.

Jack and Annie hurried through the moonlit garden back to the summer palace. They followed Wolfie up the stairway that led to the terrace.

"I'm here, Nan!" Wolfie called.

Nan ran across the terrace and grabbed him. "Oh, Wolfie! Where were you?" she asked.

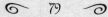

"I was in the garden! Oh, Nan, the most amazing thing—" said Wolfie.

"Not now, Wolfie, we don't have time," Nan said. She brushed off his jacket and straightened his wig.

"I love music, Nan! Jack and Annie made me love music again!" Wolfie said, pointing at Jack and Annie.

"I'm glad, good, come now," said Nan. "We have to hurry to the Hall of Mirrors! Papa's there waiting for us!" Nan pulled Wolfie toward the door.

"Jack, Annie, come with us!" Wolfie yelled over his shoulder.

"In a minute! We'll be right there!" said Annie.

As Wolfie and Nan went inside, Annie tried to smooth her clothes. The lace on her petticoat was ripped. The bottom of her dress was dirty. Her bows had come untied. The hoop of her skirt was bent. "I'm a mess," she said to Jack.

"Me too," he said. His jacket was dirty and his pants were torn. He found his wig and hat where he'd left them and scrunched them back onto his head. "But we have to look for the artists now," he said.

"What about Wolfie?" said Annie.

"Forget it. We don't have time to hang out with Wolfie," said Jack.

"But we told him we'd come," said Annie.

"We can't spend our whole lives chasing after Wolfie!" said Jack. "Because of him, we've already used up our only chance to make magic. And we haven't even started our mission yet!"

"Okay, okay," said Annie. "But we should at least say good-bye to him and Nan."

Jack sighed. "Okay. A *quick* good-bye," he said.

Jack and Annie walked across the terrace and stepped into the palace.

"Excuse me," Annie said to a servant, "where is the Hall of Mirrors?"

The servant frowned at their appearance. But he pointed to a door on the right. "Pass through the next three rooms, then through the Great Rosa Room, into the Hall of Mirrors."

"Thanks!" Jack and Annie hurried through the four rooms until they came to a large door. They opened it and peeked into the Hall of Mirrors.

Mirrors hung on the walls. The room was filled with party guests sitting in rows of chairs. Her Imperial Majesty and the imperial children sat in the front row. Wolfie was standing near the front of the room with Nan and their father.

Jack wanted to leave as quickly as possible. But Wolfie saw them and called out, "Jack! Annie! Come in!"

Jack started to slip away. But Annie pushed the door open and stepped inside. *Oh, brother,* thought Jack, following her.

"Watch me!" cried Wolfie. Then Wolfie shot away from his family and hopped in front of the crowd.

Oh, no! thought Jack. *What's he doing? Why doesn't someone grab him?*

Wolfie faced the audience. He placed his hand over his heart and bowed. Then he swept back his coattails and climbed up on a bench in front of an odd-looking piano. His short legs didn't even reach the floor.

Wolfie closed his eyes and bowed his head close to the keyboard. With just one finger he began tapping out some musical notes.

Why's everyone watching this little kid pretend to play the piano? Jack wondered. Then he realized something amazing: the simple tune Wolfie was picking out on the keyboard was the same tune the magic flute had played in the garden.

Everyone in the room seemed to hold their breath as Wolfie played. He went from tapping with one finger to tapping with two fingers and then three. As Wolfie kept tapping out notes, he didn't look like a silly six-year-old anymore. The expression on his face was thoughtful and dreamy.

Suddenly Wolfie was playing with all his fingers. His small hands flew over the black and white keys as he added to the tune of the magic flute.

Jack was stunned. He couldn't believe a little kid could make such beautiful music. The sounds from the piano were sometimes light and playful, and at other times heavy and forceful. The slow parts of Wolfie's music made Jack want to close his eyes. The lively parts made him want to bounce up and down.

Wolfie ended his concert with a great flourish. Then he stood up and bowed.

The guests jumped to their feet, smiling and laughing, clapping and yelling, "Bravo! Bravo!"

Wolfie kept bowing. The clapping and cheering would die down, but then it would start up again. As long as people clapped, Wolfie bowed.

Finally Wolfie's father stepped up to the piano. Then Wolfie seemed to turn into a little kid again. "Papa!" he said. He grabbed his father and buried his face in his father's coat. Wolfie's dad had tears on his cheeks as he hugged his son.

All the guests talked excitedly about the performance they'd just seen:

"I couldn't believe my ears!"

"I couldn't believe my eyes!"

"How did he do it? He is so young and small!"

As the party guests kept praising Wolfie, Nan walked over to Jack and Annie. "Thank you for bringing Wolfie back for his concert," she said.

"Has he been playing a long time?" Annie asked.

"Papa has been teaching him since he was three," said Nan. "And now Wolfie is even starting to write his own music. He tells Papa he hears tunes in his head—like the tune he played tonight. I have never heard that one before."

Annie smiled at Jack, and he smiled back at her. "Cool," Annie said.

A hush fell over the crowd. Her Imperial Majesty had stepped forward. She took Wolfie's hands in hers. "Thank you for your brilliant performance, Wolfgang Amadeus Mozart," she said.

As the crowd clapped wildly again, Annie looked at Jack. "Mozart!" she said.

Jack was confused. *Mozart?* He knew the name Mozart. Their piano teacher loved the music of Mozart. Their parents loved it, too. In fact, they'd once taken Annie and Jack to hear a concert of Mozart's music. Jack couldn't believe that this strange little kid was the world-famous Mozart.

The applause stopped as Her Imperial Majesty spoke to the crowd. "We have witnessed a great event here tonight. I know we will all remember it in the years to come, when our young Wolfgang Mozart brings joy to all the world with his music."

"Oh, man," Jack whispered. He looked at Annie. "Did you hear that?"

Annie smiled at him and nodded.

"Thank you again for your help," Nan said to them. She started to leave, then turned back. "Oh, I asked Papa your question about the artists living here. He said he was talking about another palace in Vienna. I am sorry."

"That's okay," said Annie. "No problem."

As Nan headed for Wolfie and her father, Annie looked at Jack. "We found our great artist," she said. "He was with us all along."

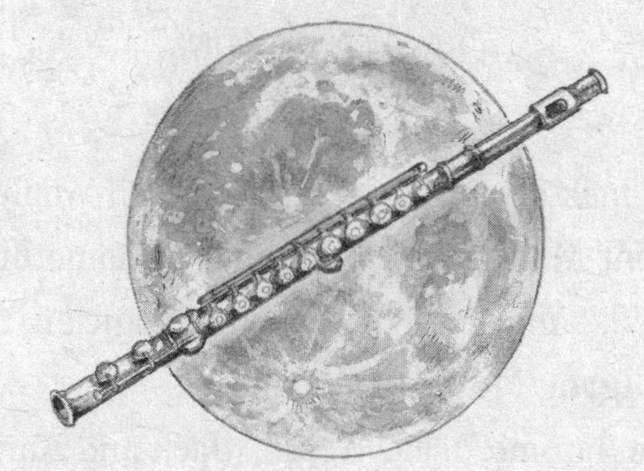

CHAPTER NINE

Me and the Clown

"Wolfgang Amadeus Mozart," said Annie.

"Yeah," Jack sighed. "And right now he's just a little kid."

"So I guess we did our mission," said Annie. "Remember what Wolfie said to Nan? He said we made him love music again. So I guess we put him back on the path to giving his gifts to the world."

"Yep, and now we can leave," said Jack. "Whew." He was ready to get out of his fancy clothes and wig and go home and have a good dinner.

"Let's go say good-bye to Wolfie," said Annie.

As Jack and Annie started toward Wolfie, Her Imperial Majesty was laughing at something he had said. “You are truly a young magician, my little Wolfgang Mozart!” she said.

“No, not me,” said Wolfie. “Jack and Annie are the true magicians!”

“Who?” said Her Imperial Majesty.

“Over there,” said Wolfie, pointing across the room. “Jack! Annie!” he called.

All eyes turned to Jack and Annie.

“Look! It’s Jack of Frog Creek!” said one of the imperial children.

Jack froze, horrified.

“Jack is a clown,” said Wolfie. “And he plays magic music on his flute. And Annie sings beautiful magic songs. I just heard them.”

“Really?” said Her Imperial Majesty. She raised her eyebrows. “Well, Jack and Annie. Perhaps you will perform for all of us here as well?”

Everyone was silent, waiting for an answer from Jack and Annie.

"Um, well, you see . . . ," Jack began.

"Sure," said Annie with a big smile. "We'd love to perform for you."

Oh, no! thought Jack.

"Yes! Sing for us! Play for us!" said Wolfie, clapping his hands. He ran to Jack and Annie and pulled them toward the front of the room.

Annie leaned close to Jack. "You play; I'll sing," she whispered.

"But the flute won't make magic anymore," Jack said out of the corner of his mouth.

"Do the best you can," whispered Annie. She smiled at the crowd.

Jack could hardly breathe. *This is worse than facing the leopard and bear!* he thought.

"Me, then you," Annie said to him.

Jack reached into his pocket and pulled out the silver flute. Annie started singing:

We came in a coach,
In a wig and a gown.

We came to Vienna,
Me and the clown.

Annie turned to Jack. As everyone watched him, he held the instrument in a playing position. He desperately hoped a little magic still lingered in the flute. He blew air over the mouthpiece.

No sound came out. All anyone could hear was Jack's huffing and puffing.

Wolfie giggled. "See! Jack's a clown!" he said.

Everyone laughed.

Okay, thought Jack, *if they want a clown, I'll be a clown.* Jack put on a goofy face. He looked into the end of the flute, as if searching for its missing sound. He jerked back his head, as if something had shot out of the flute and hit him in the eye.

Everyone laughed harder.

Jack liked hearing their laughter this time. He made a big show of wiping his eye. Then he gave Annie a silly grin.

Annie shook her head and sang:

My brother's a fool,
He's always around.
Why is it always
Me and the clown?

Jack pretended to bonk her on the head with his flute. He tried playing again, but again no sound came out. He turned the flute upside down and shook it, as if he were trying to shake out some music.

Annie rolled her eyes, to show she thought Jack was hopeless. Then she nodded at him, motioning for him to walk with her. As they moved away from the front of the room, Annie sang the last verse of her song:

It's time to go,
It's time to leave town.
Good-bye from me, and
Good-bye from the clown.

Crossing the room, Jack put the flute to his lips

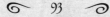

again. As he followed Annie to the door, he looked at the crowd and winked. Then he started to make up his own flute sounds. *"Tweetle-tweetle-tweetle!"* he sang. *"Toot-toot-ah-roo!"*

The audience laughed. When Jack saw Nan laughing hard, it spurred him on, and he did a little dance step. *"Peep-peep-peep-ah-lee!"* he sang, pretending to play the flute. *"Peek-peek-a-boo!"*

At the door, Jack and Annie stopped. Jack held the flute to his side and bowed. Annie curtsied at the same time. The audience laughed and clapped. Together Jack and Annie waved to the crowd.

"Bye, Wolfie!" shouted Annie. She blew kisses to him. "Keep making music!"

"Have a great life, Wolfie!" shouted Jack.

"Bye, Jack! Bye, Annie!" yelled Wolfie. "I promise I will never forget you!"

Jack bowed very low, and Annie curtsied again.

"Rise," said Her Imperial Majesty, laughing.

Jack and Annie straightened up, waved one last time, and slipped out the door.

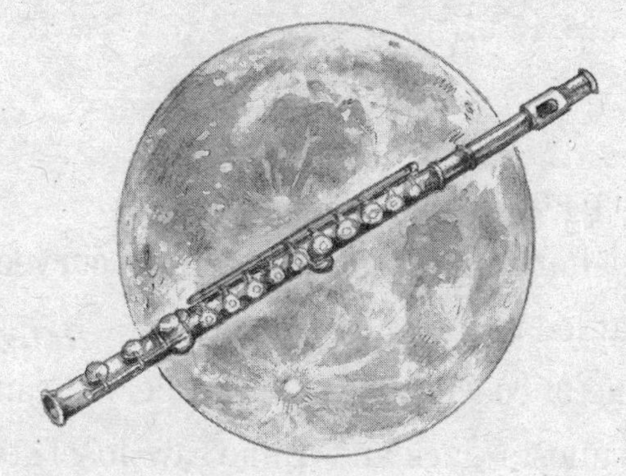

CHAPTER TEN

Joy

"Go, go!" said Jack.

Jack and Annie ran through the Great Rosa Room, through the next three rooms, and into the room off the back terrace. Then they turned and hurried to the huge party room, where the thousand candles had nearly burned out. They ran to the door that led out to the front entrance.

"We have to leave. Good night!" Annie said to the guard. "Thanks for everything!"

The guard opened the door, and they ran outside.

"Keep going!" said Jack.

They hurried down the sweeping, curved stairway that led to the giant square.

A line of coaches was parked below, waiting to pick up guests. Jack and Annie saw Josef standing by his coach. The moonlight shone on his two milk white horses.

"Josef!" shouted Annie.

Jack and Annie ran over to the coachman.

"Ah, my young friends!" he said. "How was your evening?"

"Great," said Annie. "But we have to go home now. Do you have time to take us back to the gate?"

"Indeed, it is early," said Josef. "I can take you now and then return for my employer and his family."

Josef gave Annie his hand and helped her into the coach. Then he helped Jack. Josef climbed up onto his bench and snapped the reins, and the two horses clomped over the cobblestones.

"So tell me now, young lady," said Josef, "did you have a good time at the party? What did you see and what did you do?"

"I had a great time!" said Annie. "I was received by Her Imperial Majesty. I saw a room lit with a thousand candles. I made good friends, met some zoo animals, heard a great concert, and saw a silly clown."

"Excellent," said Josef. "And you, young man?"

"I did all those things, too," said Jack. "But the clown was the best part. He knew how to make great use of his wits and his talents."

Annie laughed. Josef drove the coach through the palace gate and stopped on the cobblestone street. "Where do you need to go?" he asked.

"Oh, this is perfect," said Annie. "We can get out right here. Thank you."

Jack and Annie climbed out of the coach and looked up at Josef.

"Thank you, Josef!" said Annie.

"Yeah, thanks a lot for the ride," said Jack.

"You two are very mysterious," said Josef. "You appeared out of the twilight and now you disappear into the moonlight."

"We're magicians," said Annie.

"It would seem so," said Josef, smiling. He tipped his hat. "Well, I had better return now. Good night, my young friends."

"Good night, Josef," said Jack and Annie.

Josef flicked the reins, and the milk white horses clomped back toward the palace gates.

"Nice guy," said Jack. "Let's go."

Jack and Annie ran to the trees that lined the cobblestone street. "There!" said Annie. She grabbed the rope ladder.

Annie started up to the tree house. Jack followed her. When they got inside, they looked out the window at the full moon shining over Vienna, Austria.

"Good-bye, Wolfie," said Annie.

"Good luck, kid," said Jack.

Then Jack picked up the envelope from their

invitation. He pointed at the words *Frog Creek.* "I wish we could go there!" he said.

The tree house started to spin.

It spun faster and faster.

Then everything was still.

Absolutely still.

♪ ♪ ♪

Jack opened his eyes. "Ahhh," he sighed with relief. They were back in the Frog Creek woods. They were wearing their own clothes again. Jack was holding the magic flute.

"Ready?" asked Annie.

"Totally," said Jack.

Jack carefully laid the flute in a corner of the tree house. Then he and Annie climbed down the rope ladder and started for home.

Jack was in such a good mood, he nearly bounced through the woods. The sun was going down, dappling the ground with lovely light. The air was soft and smelled like new leaves. Jack knew a good dinner was waiting for them at home.

When Jack and Annie came out of the woods, they took off running down the street. They crossed their yard, scrambled onto the porch, and banged through the front door.

"We're back!" Annie called.

"Just in time," their dad said from the kitchen. "Dinner's in a few minutes."

"Quick, before we eat . . . ," Jack said to Annie. He led her over to the computer. He sat down and typed in one word: *Mozart.*

There were 48,400,207 entries.

"Whoa!" said Jack. He clicked the first one. He read aloud:

> **Wolfgang Amadeus Mozart was the most famous child musician in history. He performed all over Europe for many years. As Mozart grew up, he composed more than six hundred pieces of music. For over two hundred years, his music has brought joy to the world.**

"*Yes!*" said Annie.

As Jack scrolled down, three words leapt out at him. He gasped. "Listen to this!" he said. And then he read to Annie:

> **Mozart's last great opera was called *The Magic Flute*.**

Annie smiled at Jack. "Wolfie kept his promise," she said. "He never forgot us."

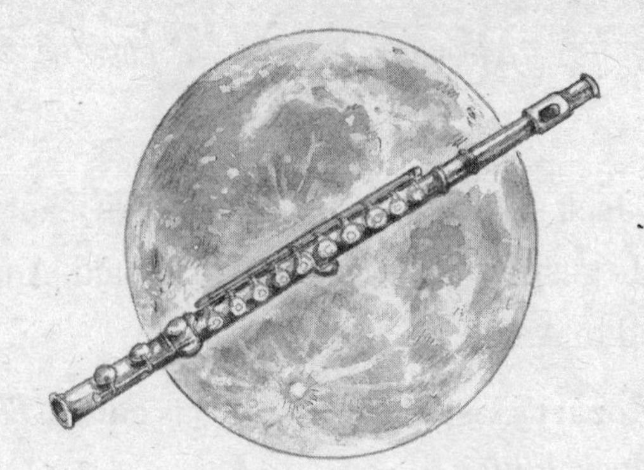

More Facts About Mozart and His Time

Born in Austria in 1756, Mozart was baptized Johannes Chrysostomus Wolfgangus Theophilus Mozart. When Mozart was three years old, his father, Leopold, began teaching him to play the organ, the violin, and the harpsichord (an early piano-like instrument). Mozart started to write his first musical compositions when he was only five.

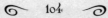

In October 1762, Leopold took Mozart and his sister, Maria Anna (also called Nannerl), to Vienna to play for the Empress Maria Theresa

and her court at her summer palace, known as Schönbrunn Palace. According to a letter from his father, during the visit the young Mozart clambered onto the lap of the empress and hugged and kissed her. The only time he did not behave like a small child was when he sat at the harpsichord to play. His genius then stunned everyone in the court.

For the next three years, Mozart and Nannerl toured the capitals of Europe as child wonders. Nannerl was considered to be as talented as her brother. But this changed when she and Mozart grew older and he began performing his own compositions. Today many consider Mozart the best classical composer who ever lived.

The summer palace of Empress Maria Theresa actually had one of the first zoos in the world. It was built in 1752 by her husband, Emperor Franz Stephan, who had a great interest in natural history. The zoo at first housed mostly exotic waterfowl. But over the years, more and more wild animals were brought there from expeditions all over the world. In 1828, the arrival of the first giraffe caused a huge sensation. Today the Schönbrunn Zoo is still a favorite tourist spot in Vienna.

Don't miss Magic Tree House® #42
(A Merlin Mission)
A Good Night for Ghosts

Jack and Annie are searching for another artist who can bring happiness to millions of people. Who will they find among the ghosts of New Orleans?

Mary Pope Osborne is the award-winning author of many novels, picture books, story collections, and nonfiction books. Her bestselling Magic Tree House series has been translated into many languages around the world. Highly recommended by parents and educators everywhere, the series introduces young readers to different cultures and times in history, as well as to the world's legacy of ancient myth and storytelling. Mary Pope Osborne is married to Will Osborne, a co-author of many of the Magic Tree House Research Guides and librettist and lyricist for *Magic Tree House: The Musical*, a theatrical adaptation of the series. They live in northwestern Connecticut with their dogs—Joey, Mr. Bezo, and Little Bear. You can visit Mary, Will, and their three dogs on the Web at www.marypopeosborne.com.

Sal Murdocca is best known for his amazing work on the Magic Tree House series. He has written and/or illustrated over two hundred children's books, including *Dancing Granny* by Elizabeth Winthrop, *Double Trouble in Walla Walla* by Andrew Clements, and *Big Numbers* by Edward Packard. He has taught writing and illustration at the Parsons School of Design in New York. He is the librettist for a children's opera and has recently completed his second short film. Sal Murdocca is an avid runner, hiker, and bicyclist. He has often bicycle-toured in Europe and has had many one-man shows of his paintings from these trips. He lives and works with his wife, Nancy, in New City, New York.